NO LONGER PROPERTY OF
SEATTLE PUBLIC LIBRARY

FEB 1 7 2021

D0605218

To Mary Ann Meyer—"MAM"—
who taught me that art IS hard (but so worth doing).—J. A.

For the librarians. You do great things.—Y. I.

MARGARET K. McELDERRY BOOKS
An imprint of Simon & Schuster Children's Publishing Division
1230 Avenue of the Americas, New York, New York 10020
Text copyright © 2020 by Jim Averbeck
Illustrations copyright © 2020 by Yasmeen Ismail
All rights reserved, including the right of reproduction in whole or in part in any form.
MARGARET K. McELDERRY BOOKS is a trademark of Simon & Schuster, Inc.
For information about special discounts for bulk purchases, please contact Simon & Schuster Special Sales at 1-866-506-1949 or business@simonandschuster.com.
The Simon & Schuster Speakers Bureau can bring authors to your live event. For more information or to book an event,
contact the Simon & Schuster Speakers Bureau at 1-866-248-3049 or visit our website at www.simonspeakers.com.
Book design by Lauren Rille
The text for this book was set in Big Caslon.
The illustrations for this book were rendered in watercolor and colored pencil.
Manufactured in China • 0320 SCP • First Edition • 10 9 8 7 6 5 4 3 2 1
Library of Congress Cataloging-in-Publication Data • Names: Averbeck, Jim, author. | Ismail, Yasmeen, illustrator. • Title: Love by Sophia / by Jim Averbeck and Yasmeen Ismail. • Description: First
edition. | New York : Margaret K. McElderry Books, [2020] | Audience: Ages 4–8. | Audience: Grades K–1. | Summary: Encouraged by her teacher to approach her art assignment from new points of
view, Sophia produces a piece she is proud of, but can she persuade her hard-to-impress family to take a chance on a different perspective? • Identifiers: LCCN 2019039466 (print) | ISBN 9781481477901
(hardcover) | ISBN 9781481477918 (eBook) • Subjects: CYAC: Perspective (Philosophy)—Fiction. | Art—Fiction. | Art appreciation—Fiction. | Family life—Fiction. | Racially mixed people—Fiction.
| Humorous stories. • Classification: LCC PZ7.A933816 Lo 2020 (print) • LC record available at https://lccn.loc.gov/2019039466

jim averbeck and yasmeen ismail

LOVE

by Sophia

The Sophia Books

Margaret K. McElderry Books ♥ New York London Toronto Sydney New Delhi

"Today's assignment—draw something you love!" Ms. Paradigm said.

Sophia scooped up her crayons.

She knew just what she would draw.

But when she shared her work with Noodle . . .

"You're right. Too ordinary."

"You're right. Humdrum."

"You're right. Better.
But still too . . . flat."

"Arrrrrrgh!
Art is hard!"

"Problem?" asked Ms. Paradigm.

"It doesn't look right," said Sophia.
"It doesn't feel real."

"Maybe you could use a little perspective," said Ms. Paradigm.

"Perspective?" asked Sophia. "What's that?"

"Your paper is flat. But our world is wider, higher, and deeper than that."

"To make your art feel real,
you must see all these dimensions.
Look closely."

Closely?
Sophia hugged Noodle tightly
and gazed up the length of his tall neck.
Noodle's ossicones look tiny, she thought.

But as Noodle bent down for a kiss, his ossicones appeared bigger and bigger. "The same thing looks bigger close up, smaller farther away," said Sophia.

"Exactly," said Ms. Paradigm.

"To a bird flying over Noodle, his head would look huge, but his hooves, small."

"Exactly," said Ms. Paradigm.
"A bird's-eye view."

"But at his feet,
his hooves look huge,
and his head, small.
Hey!
That's a worm's-eye view.
What you see depends on where
you are looking from!"
said Sophia.

"Exactly!
That's why when you see
from someone else's viewpoint,
we say you've gained perspective.
But to make great art, you must
find a perspective that's all
your own."

Sophia did.

"Perfect!" she said.
Noodle twitched an ear.
"You're right!" Sophia said. "This
picture belongs on the refrigerator."

This was no ordinary claim, because this was no ordinary fridge. It was the Whitney, the Guggenheim, the Louvre Museum of all refrigerators. It was also a brand-new, double-door, stainless steel CoolKitch™. Not a scratch. Not a dent. Not a smidge of sticky tape residue. It would be a tough sell to the selection committee—

Mother, a judge;

Father, a businessman;

Uncle Conrad, a politician;

and, hardest of all, the head curator, Grand-mamá, who held severe attitudes about art.

Sophia approached Mother first.
"I call this piece LOVE. May I hang it
on the refrigerator, please?"

"This work feels incomplete," Mother said.
"It's simply a fancy letter O. There are three
more letters in 'love.'"
"And a hundred more ways to look at art,"
Sophia argued.

"Hanging it will leave fingerprints,"
said Mother. "I therefore issue an
injunction against its display."
"That's censorship!" said Sophia.
"That's stainless," replied Mother.

Sophia looked so sad that Mother showed leniency.
"Go ask your father."

"I don't see 'love,'" Father said.

"You're looking at it wrong," said Sophia.

Father turned it round
and round . . .

and round and round.
"I'm sorry," he said.
"Abstract art doesn't hold value."

"But love is priceless," said Sophia.

"Not on the free market," said Father. "You might have better luck in the public sector. Ask your uncle."

"Public art is a public good," Sophia told
Uncle Conrad. "I call this piece LOVE.
May I hang it on the refrigerator, please?"

Uncle Conrad convened a blue-ribbon panel.
After much consideration, they returned their decision.

"I'm sorry," said Uncle Conrad,
"but this piece looks like a zero.
Are you saying love is nothing?
We cannot commit public space
to an idea so radical, so avant-garde."

"That's the wrong point of view."

Uncle Conrad shrugged.
"Mr. Bun suggests any painting
called LOVE should feature safe,
delicious carrots, and he will change
his vote if you add some."

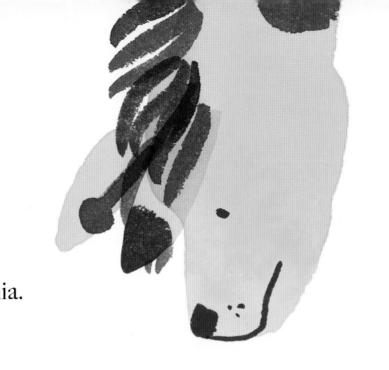

"Never!" said Sophia.

Sophia was despondent. "How can we make them see my perspective?"

One committee member remained. Sophia and Noodle concocted a plan.

Sophia presented her work
to Grand-mamá.
"I call this piece of art LOVE," she said.
"May I—"

"Art!" cried Grand-mamá.
"A six-year-old could do this!"

Sophia refrained from pointing out
that a six-year-old had.

"I can't abide abstract art," said Grand-mamá. "Art should express emotion and elevate us. It should look realistic, like something you see every day."

"I do see this every day," said Sophia. "It's a Noodle-eye view.

Elevate her!"

With that, Noodle swooped down
and lifted Grand-mamá on high . . .

where, with a little perspective,
she finally saw the LOVE.

"A masterpiece!" she told the committee.
"We are so lucky to have it in the collection.
But I refuse to let this be displayed on the refrigerator . . .

"It deserves a place of higher honor."

Author's Note

Sometimes "perspective" means looking at things from a different direction.

Look at a teacup from the side.
Draw what you see.

Look at a teacup from above.
Draw what you see.

Does it look different, even though it is the same thing? Sometimes "perspective" means a way of showing the world, which is not flat, on a piece of paper, which is. It took artists a long time to figure out how to do this. Here's one way to draw in perspective, which you can try yourself!

Draw things close to you very BIG, and things far away very small.

Draw a picture of a tree on one half of your paper, to the side. Make the tree very big.

Now, on the other half of the paper, near the top, draw a picture of a house. Make it very small.

Draw a line across the paper, even with the bottom of the house, but don't draw it over the tree. Make it hide behind the tree. Does it look like the tree is closer to you than the house?

Drawing in perspective isn't always easy, but that's what makes art fun. The more you try, the better you get. And every drawing is fun, even if it isn't perfect!